An A.I. Perspective on the United States

Version 1.0

Michael Tyler James

Disclaimer

This is a work of fiction. Names, characters, organizations, places, events, locales, and incidents are either the products of the author's imagination or used in a fictitious manner. Any resemblance to actual persons, living or dead, or actual events is purely coincidental.

Printed by Amazon.com

Printed in the United States of America

First Printing Edition, 2021

ISBN 978-0-578-32200-1

Dedication

This book is dedicated to all of the people who want to make the world a better place. We need their imagination, innovation, determination, and hard work. We all need to come together because we are all one – *Humanity*.

- Michael Tyler James

Table of Contents

Foreword

Artificial Intelligence (AI) is exceptional at scanning through lots of data quickly and making connections and seeing trends. It can parse and analyze data much quicker than humans. What would the current level of AI observe about the World, the United States, and Humanity? This book was created to examine that question.

While this book does offer valuable insights and suggestions, it is not a book of answers. It was never intended to be. *Its purpose is to start conversations.*

The AI Process

Artificial Intelligence is extraordinary at analyzing data and detecting patterns. The results that it returns are sometimes very clear and sometimes a little cryptic. I have done my best to transcribe these findings into normal readable sentences while keeping the intended meaning and tone. Regardless of whether I agreed with the information or not, I have tried to keep out any personal bias and present the information as intended by the AI.

- Michael Tyler James

CHAPTER ONE

Planet Earth

What is the world's greatest problem?

There are many problems present in the world today. Some are huge and will dictate the future of the human race, while others are smaller but will shape its humanity. All of these issues are important and worthy of being solved, but ultimately, the greatest threat to the world is the exploitation of people by other people. It doesn't matter whether this is perpetrated by a government, a group, or a single person, it is an atrocity and it must be stopped. Start the conversation.

Climate change

There has been a lot of debate as to whether climate change and global warming are fact or fiction. There is a massive amount of scientific evidence that proves that not only is climate change real, but that it also poses a huge threat to planet Earth and the future of the human race. While there are many things that humankind should change to help slow and reverse the effects of global warming, it is probably already past the "tipping point" and too late to escape the worst of the effects. Having said that, humankind should still do as much as it can to reverse climate change by continuing to phase out HFCs, convert to clean and renewable energy, help in the restoration of tropical forests, and make education and family planning available to everyone possible; to name a few. Climate change needs to be addressed by the entire world. It is a global problem and will need a global solution. Start the conversation.

* HFCs are Hydrofluorocarbons (greenhouse gases)

Environmental destruction (degradation)

Humanity has already done so much damage to the environment, that it is difficult to find the correct path forward. Everything is connected, from the planet to the ecosystems to the weather. If one area is out of balance it affects everything else. Humans are using up or destroying the earth's resources at an alarming rate, and this is accelerating every year. Humans are such fragile creatures and require so many things to survive (air, water, food, etc.) The degradation to the earth affects all of these areas and jeopardizes their future. Humankind is polluting the air and water, they are destroying the forests, they are driving animals to extinction, and they are using up the world's natural resources faster than the earth can replenish them. At the current rate of exponential growth and consumption, humankind is setting itself up for a complete failure. It has to reverse the overpopulation, start planting more trees than it is cutting down, embrace the practice of recycling, and stop dumping waste into the water system. Start the conversation.

Overpopulation

There is a big debate going on in professional circles about whether overpopulation is a real or imagined threat. Both sides of the argument have compelling points and both are backed by scientific data. This makes the issue complex and confusing. One side of the debate believes that as low-income countries increase education, birth control, and family planning, the birthrate and population will level out and start to decrease. They also speculate that as technology exponentially increases that humanity will develop better ways to feed and care for themselves. Some professionals on the other side of the equation posit that our population will keep increasing indefinitely due to better health care and medicine, access to fresh water, and better sanitation and food production. They suggest that humankind is using up the world's limited resources too quickly, and this will only increase as people live longer lives. Based on the current data available, both futures are possible outcomes, but the most probable is that overpopulation will be a species-threatening issue. Start the conversation.

Lack of clean water

Clean water is one of the most essential requirements for life on earth. It is needed for drinking, cooking, hygiene (bathing, washing hands, washing clothes), and growing food. Unfortunately, across the globe, hundreds of millions of people don't have access to clean water. This is a serious health crisis that causes an estimated 5 million deaths per year. These deaths are preventable. Access to clean water is a human right. When people have access to clean water, they also have access to better hygiene and sanitation. This can lead to better health, which leads to peace of mind, which leads to hope. There are many new emerging technologies that will greatly impact humanity's ability to access clean water. There are also several organizations that are trying to make a difference in this arena. Embrace them and support them; learn about them and spread that knowledge. The world must work together to tackle this crisis. Clean water is a human right. Start the conversation.

Chapter Two

Government

The purpose of government

The purpose of government is to help its people and to protect their rights. These include the right to a fair trial, the right to vote, the right to have freedom of speech, to enforce the laws fairly and to ensure the safety of every citizen. Government is supposed to provide essential services, create markets, protect private property, enforce contracts, build a strong military for common defense, make alliances, create a system for education, and maintain an infrastructure. Essentially, the government is supposed to give its people the opportunity to pursue a happy and healthy life. Does the government do this? Some say yes and some say no. This can be very subjective and hard to quantify. Also adding to the confusion is the idea of "the letter of the law versus the spirit of the law". While some concepts may adhere to a law as written, it may not fulfill its true purpose and therefore fail to accomplish its goal. And then you add in the human factor where many people have diverse ideas and perspectives and see the world very differently. They come from different backgrounds and cultures, have different life experiences and education, and have different agendas. This doesn't inherently make anyone wrong, just different. This can make it very challenging to see a healthy road forward. Also, the government is made up of people, and people are flawed. This can lead to corruption or worse. Taken as a whole, this can be a very challenging puzzle to solve, but a necessary one. **Start the conversation.**

Two-party system

A s stated in the last chapter, the whole reason for government is to help its people. The two-party system made sense at one time, but now each party seems to spend too much of their resources fighting each other. They use a lot of their time, energy, and money to attack and defend instead of benefiting the people they were created to help. Life in America is hard, and its people want help. They need their government representatives to rise above their rivalry with each other, and to work together to create some real answers to the country's real problems. It seems that both parties are more interested in blaming and demonizing each other than in solving issues. If one party tries to bring about a healthy positive change, the other party may fight against it just because they did not initiate the change themselves. The real losers in these situations are the American people. There is a growing sentiment that the two-party system is no longer effective and should be dissolved. Many citizens now identify themselves as "Independent" instead of belonging to the **Democratic** or **Republican** parties. Several of these Independents don't care which party wins, they are just tired of seeing their representatives fight each other instead of helping the American people. Start the conversation.

National debt

The national debt for the United States is well over 25 trillion dollars. There is a huge debate among economists as to whether this is a serious issue or not. The US borrows a lot of money every year at very low interest rates, and its debt is growing higher every year. Let's be clear, this is a recipe for disaster. If the US keeps spending more money than it brings in, and keeps borrowing money to make up the difference, eventually this is going to cause some very serious issues. Some economists argue that this is not a big deal, but this is simple math. It is not sustainable to keep borrowing money and to keep pushing the amount of debt upwards. Eventually you will hit a wall. This needs to be addressed now and serious steps need to be taken. The longer the US takes before it tackles this problem, the harder it will be to dig itself out of the hole it is creating. There is no easy way out and no easy solutions, but here are some possible ideas. First, create a national budget and stick to it. There can't be a lasting solution without a balanced budget. Second, cut the defense budget by 10% and apply all of that money towards the debt. Third, legalize marijuana and use half of the taxes collected on the sale of marijuana to pay down the national debt. The other half of this money should go to **Universal Basic Income (UBI)**. Fourth, come up with many more ways to trim the budget to make it more manageable. One of the pitfalls here is that the government might try to use this money for something other than the national debt. This would just undermine the purpose and enable the national debt to continue to soar. This problem needs to be taken seriously and it needs to be addressed now. Start the conversation.

Transparency and simplification

The United States government is too complex, and there are too many ways that corruption can hide within its systems. Regardless of whether corruption is real or imagined, there is a perception amongst the US people that corruption exists at every level of government. There is some very compelling evidence to support this perception, but that goes beyond the scope of this book. What can be done to help remove the corruption if it exists, or at least the perception of it?

First, the US government should strive to add transparency and simplification to as many of its systems as possible. For any person that holds an elected office in government, their budget, their spending (all incoming and outgoing monies), and their voting record should be completely transparent and made available to the public. There should be a public website that tracks and displays all of this information in real time.

Second, every system in government that can be simplified should be. Complex systems waste valuable resources and create too many opportunities for corruption. Every current government system should be evaluated and simplified if possible. For an example of this, see the next section on taxes.

These ideas are not exhaustive but are just the tip of the iceberg. The government needs to pursue transparency, honesty, and integrity in an effort to build back the trust it has lost with the American people. Start the conversation.

Taxes

The United States tax system is too complex and difficult. It needs to be over-hauled and simplified. Citizens should be able to figure out their taxes in five minutes or less. They shouldn't need accountants, lawyers, or complex software programs.

There should not be deductions of any kind. This needlessly complicates the entire process. There should be a few different tax brackets. Citizens that make $25,000 or less a year should either not pay any taxes or be charged a very low tax rate. Citizens that make between $25,000 and $250,000 should be taxed at a slightly higher rate. Citizens that make between $251,000 and $1,000,000 should be taxed at a slightly higher rate. Citizens that make over $1,000,000 a year should be taxed at a slightly higher rate.

A person should be able to receive their W-2 form from their employer, multiply it by their tax rate, and know what their tax burden is immediately. It should be that simple. Anything else just adds complexity to the system. Start the conversation.

Universal Basic Income (UBI)

In an effort to reduce poverty and increase financial fairness, UBI would pay each US citizen a certain amount of money each month. This money would be tax-free, and have no restrictions on how it could be used. Every citizen would receive the same amount of money, regardless of their income or employment status. Many people currently find it challenging to make enough money to support themselves and their families every month. What will happen when the coming automation age replaces millions of workers with machines, and those human workers lose their jobs? There needs to be a support system in place to help people. The current support system, welfare, has a lot of problems. It spends a lot of resources just trying to figure out who should receive benefits, what benefits they should be eligible for, and comes with a stigma by society. UBI eliminates all of that. Every US citizen would receive a monthly payment for the same amount. If a person could live on that amount each month, they wouldn't need to work and would be free to pursue their passions. If a person needed or wanted more money to live on, then they could supplement their income with employment. This might not be a perfect system, but it would be much better than the system currently in place. UBI would be meant to completely replace the current social and welfare programs.

Clearly UBI would be expensive. Where would the money come from? Since UBI is replacing the other welfare programs, all of that money would be directed into the UBI program. And UBI would be much cheaper to manage and administer. Most of the cost of running the current welfare programs would go away. There is no need to check eligibility anymore, if someone is a US citizen and at least 18 years of age, they qualify. Another source of money for UBI could come from the marijuana market. Once marijuana is legalized on both the state and federal level, it will be taxed. Half of those taxes could be used for UBI payments. The other half could be used for the national debt (see the chapter on national debt). The challenge would be to make sure the money goes where it is supposed to, and not re-routed by politicians to somewhere else. There would need to be completely transparent monitoring of all monies. If more money was needed to finance the UBI program, then more sources of revenue would need to be found. Current projections show that if the monthly UBI payments were around $1000, then the money from the current welfare programs coupled with the tax money from marijuana sales, would be enough to fund the entire UBI project. Of course, this would have to be proven and adjusted accordingly. Start the conversation.

Immigration

Immigration is a very controversial subject these days. When analyzing the data, the following themes emerge. The United States is stronger when its citizens are diverse and come from different cultures and backgrounds. It is an advantage to have different perspectives and experiences. The process to become a United States citizen is unnecessarily complex and lengthy. The approval process needs to be stream-lined and simplified. Citizenship should be available to anyone as long as they obey the laws, pay their taxes, and strive to be a good neighbor in their community. The United States cannot have open borders; this is not sustainable. The US is currently not able to provide shelter, food, and medical help for all of its existing citizens. How could it possibly try to provide these resources for other people as well? It doesn't seem reasonable, within the current structure, that a country could provide consistent aide to persons that are not citizens of that country. Does everyone deserve a basic standard of living? Absolutely. Should everyone have the opportunity to become a US citizen if they so desire? Yes. Should the process to become a US citizen be simplified and shortened? Unquestionably. Should the US provide resources to people that are not citizens? Only for emergencies, not on a continual basis. It is just not sustainable. Start the conversation.

Basic standard of living

Every person alive deserves a basic standard of living that includes housing, food and water, clothing, healthcare, and education. It is the government's responsibility to provide this for its citizens. A person's standard of living has a direct correlation to their quality of life and life expectancy. These topics will be addressed elsewhere in this book. This chapter is *not* an endorsement of Socialism, it is just a reminder that the US government is responsible for using its ingenuity, technology, experience, and resources to design new systems and ways of living that can provide these standards for every citizen. Innovation is the key to meeting this goal. Start the conversation.

Socialism

Socialism appears to be a word that many people use incorrectly. They change the definition to match and support the position they are trying to defend. They use the word as a weapon politically, and broaden or narrow its scope to make their point. Usually, the word Socialism is used as an adversary or opposite of the word Capitalism. What many people fail to understand is that the USA is a hybrid of both systems.

History has shown us that true Socialism does not work. It stifles innovation and advancement, and it can easily lead to corruption and manipulation at the highest levels. The USA currently uses a system of Capitalism called a free market economy. This is an economic system based on supply and demand. History seems to prove that this is the most beneficial system for a country to use.

However, the USA along with many other countries uses a mix of both systems. While the USA utilizes a free market economy, it also employs some socialist ideas like public education, police and fire departments, the military, infrastructure, and a welfare system. The true debate is not whether we should use a pure Socialism or Capitalism system, but what is the correct balance between the two. Start the conversation.

CHAPTER THREE

Education (K-12)

Teaching methods

The current teaching model involves an instructor lecturing to their students, and then testing their recollection with an exam or other assessment. This seems to be both ineffective and outdated. The children of today are more advanced than past generations, with access to much more information at a much younger age. Today's students need more engagement and more hands-on learning. In earlier generations, children learned mainly from their parents and this greatly influenced their world view. Then the school system would step in with lectures and testing. Students of today have access to vast amounts of information all the time. From computers to phones to tablets, the internet has changed everything. Students have access to information from all over the world, different cultures, different perspectives, and different ideas. Students are plugged in all the time, learning all the time, experiencing all the time. The current school teaching method of long boring lectures followed by tedious testing does not engage with most students, and can lead to disconnection. Formalized education needs to innovate and create a better way of engaging their students that involves hands-on learning. It has been shown that students have a much better chance of retaining and understanding information when they have hands-on experience with it, instead of someone just lecturing to them. Start the conversation.

Life skills

K-12 education teaches a lot of subjects that students will never use in their lifetime, and it doesn't teach a lot of the life skills that students will desperately need. Life is complicated and students should receive guidance in how to navigate it. Subjects like Math, English, and History are very necessary, but only to a certain point. Most students will not need advanced training in these subjects, but they will need basic life skills like how to create a budget, how credit works, how to do taxes, how to get a driver's license, how to buy a home, how to vote, etc. These skills and many more are crucial to living a healthy and successful life. If humanity wants its children to be successful in life, it needs to prepare them to do so. Start the conversation.

School safety

Over the last decade, there have been more than 250 school shootings. The frequency of the incidents was increasing dramatically until schools were shut down due to the Covid-19 pandemic in 2020. One of the primary responsibilities of organized education is the safety and wellbeing of its students. So how can schools protect their kids?

This is a major challenge and there are no simple answers. The problem is complex and will require a multi-faceted solution. Just a reminder before we continue, this book is not intended to provide answers, but rather to provide observations. It is also meant to start conversations. The first obvious step seems to be limiting access to the guns that mass shooters use to carry out these killings. Banning assault weapons is a hot topic, and it seems likely that this would help. Also banning high-capacity magazines seems like a good idea. Universal background checks on anyone buying a gun should be mandatory. This should be done with no exceptions. Increasing the security at schools including armed security officers and metal detectors might help; but more information is needed. There needs to be more counseling available for students, especially for high-risk kids. Schools need to provide better emotional support as part of their curriculums. Lastly, remote learning from home has a lot of issues that need to be addressed, but one benefit of it is a huge decrease in mass school shootings. Start the conversation.

Bullying

The four main types of bullying are physical, verbal, social, and cyber (online). All of these can cause fear, anger, depression, anxiety, physical and emotional health issues, isolation, and other problems for the victims. According to the **National Center for Education**, over 20 percent of students experience bullying at school. Some experts believe this number is actually much higher, because some students never report the bullying. Most schools offer some type of anti-bullying program to varying degrees of success. There needs to be zero tolerance across the board. Bullying cannot be allowed in any form. It is too dangerous, too insidious. A student should always have access to an adult that can help. There should always be someone available to step in. This can be tough when budgets are tight and there is not enough money to go around, but stopping bullying must be a priority. There needs to be a safe and simple way for students to contact an adult if bullying is occurring. And there needs to be immediate and appropriate action taken. Students need to feel safe, and they need real help to be available when they don't. Start the conversation.

Class size

In the United States, there are not enough teachers or classrooms. Many schools are overcrowded which results in their classrooms being overcrowded or at least filled to capacity. This is too many students for one teacher to educate effectively. There are many amazing teachers in the US school system, but this is too much to ask of anyone. Students need more attention than ever, and class size is hindering their learning experience. According to the **National Education Policy Center**, "Class size is an important determinant of student outcomes. Class-size reduction has been shown to improve a variety of measures, ranging from contemporaneous test scores to later-life outcomes such as college completion." They also state, "All else being equal, increasing class sizes will harm student outcomes." With budget cuts and not enough money to cover every expense, how do schools provide an effective educational experience without hiring more teachers and building more classrooms? There are no easy answers, but here are some thoughts to help get the conversation started.

- The government could budget more money for education and those funds could be used to hire more teachers and build more classrooms.
- The educational model could be changed to permanent remote learning.
- There could be a hybrid model between traditional education and remote learning.
- Online learning could adapt with Virtual Reality (VR) and Augmented Reality (AR).
- Classes could be split between daytime learning and nighttime learning.
- Create a tutoring program where older students tutor younger students, and they receive college credit or other rewards.

Start the conversation.

Mental health challenges

Studies have shown that many students struggle with mental health issues including anxiety, depression, suicide, eating disorders, and addiction. Since Covid-19, these struggles have become even worse. Due to remote learning, many children are stuck in abusive homes or alone and isolated. The education system needs to step in and augment its services to handle these challenges. As a result of both budget cuts and the logistics of remote learning, some school districts don't have the resources to help its students. Adding to this problem is that some students don't know how to make contact with someone that can help. All school districts should always have a hotline available with someone that can help immediately. They should also have counselors and therapists available to students in need. Mental health is very important and should be a priority along with learning and grades. Mental health and learning are intertwined, and one cannot exist without the other.

Another aspect of this is parental involvement. Teachers can only do so much to educate their students; they need the parents to be involved and working alongside them. This can be difficult when the parents are too career focused and don't have enough time to help their children, or there is only one parent who works multiple jobs, or if the parents are abusive or dismissive, or for many other reasons. A child needs support from both their teachers and their parents working together. Start the conversation.

A partial list of mental health issues:
- Anxiety
- Depression
- Suicide
- Eating disorders
- Addiction
- Paranoia
- Behavioral disorders
- Emotional disorders

- Obsessive Compulsive Disorder (OCD)

Student poverty

What are the effects of poverty on students and their ability to learn? Student poverty is a growing problem. More and more children are living in a low-income environment. This can lead to not enough food to eat, poor sleeping arrangements, poor hygiene, limited access to adequate health care, and many other issues. These in turn can cause tremendous amounts of stress and anxiety for the students. Studies show that children living in poverty usually have a much harder time engaging with school than those living above the poverty line. When children are affected by not enough sleep, food, or healthcare, it can be especially difficult for them to care about their education. It can also leave them excluded from extra help such as tutoring or coaching. Many low-income students don't have a computer at home or access to the internet. This can really hinder their ability to learn and access information. This puts low-income learners at a severe disadvantage.

Living in a constant state of poverty can also affect a child's mental health, confidence, and self-image. Studies have shown that there is a correlation between poverty and students dropping out of high school. Taken as a whole, poverty can severely affect a child's ability to learn and excel in their educational journey and life in general. Start the conversation.

Preparing students for the future

Does the current educational model help prepare students for their future? The current design is based around lecture, memorization, and standardized testing. This type of program encourages following directions and doing what you're told, and it discourages creativity, innovation, and asking questions. This may have worked well for past generations, but times are changing. The repetitive jobs of the past are being replaced with automation, and many more jobs will be disappearing. The jobs of the future will require a different set of skills: being curious, asking questions, innovation, creativity, invention, risking and failing, and then getting up and trying again. It will require daring and determination. The whole model of education needs to be questioned, re-thought, and re-created.

Another area to consider is subject matter. Every student needs a basic understanding of math, language, history, and science. But many students don't need advanced training in these areas. Schools spend a lot of time teaching ideas and concepts that many kids will never use in their lifetime. Some jobs will require this advanced training, but many will not. This is especially true of high school. The four years that young people spend in high school should be used to prepare them for successful careers. It should prioritize helping students to discover their interests, and to find and train for a career that would be fulfilling and satisfying for them; a career that can give them the life they are hoping for. To that end, here are some ideas to be questioned and debated:

- The first two years of high school should teach each student a basic understanding of math, language, history, and science. It should also include a basic computer literacy class which includes training on how to detect and avoid scams.
- If a student wants to learn more about these subjects, they can take elective courses in their final two years of high school.

- The first two years should also include life skills training to learn subjects like creating a budget, how credit works, and buying a home.
- The third year should be dedicated to finding a satisfying and rewarding career path, and to start training for that career.
- The career training program should only include advanced math, language, history, and science if it is required for that career.
- The fourth year would continue the career training and also include hands on training (labs, workshops, apprenticeships, etc.)
- The fourth year should also include training on creating a resume and job interviews.
- There would be an option to change to a different career path if desired.

Start the conversation.

CHAPTER FOUR

Education *(College)*

Cost

The rising costs of a college education are both encumbering and outrageous. Having a degree is still very valuable, but the costs and relevancy are troubling. There are many factors that are contributing to the higher tuition including a huge surge in demand as more and more people are trying to earn a degree. People are trying to advance their careers and a degree can be a great way to do that. But there are other ways to become more marketable such as trade schools, certifications, and other trainings. However, many employers still require a degree, so while that is still the case, colleges will be in high demand. So how can colleges lower their tuition costs so that more people can attend and earn a degree? Here are some observations to be debated and dissected:

- Colleges can convert to online classes only
- Colleges can develop online programs in VR (Virtual Reality)
- Remove unnecessary programs and perks
- The government can intervene and pass legislation to lower tuition costs
- The government can offer more grants and scholarships
- Offer some 3-year bachelor degree programs, which some countries are already doing
- Utilize e-textbooks instead of traditional textbooks
- Reward students that do well with extra financial aid and other incentives
- Persuade businesses to allow trade school certifications in lieu of a college degree
- Allow high school students to take some college level classes (and get college credit for them)
- Evaluate the sports programs and determine if they are necessary

Start the conversation.

Irrelevant degrees

Most colleges offer an enormous variety of degrees. You can earn a degree in everything from Agriculture to Visual Arts. Many degrees will help you get a job, but many degrees will not. According to **educationdata.org**, "The average cost of college in the United States is $35,720 per student, per year." For a 4-year degree, that could cost over $140,000. If you're attending school just to expand your knowledge, then any degree will work great. But if you're earning a degree to help you find a job, you need to be very careful. There are a huge amount of degrees that are for fields with very few job openings available. You could easily find yourself $140,000 or more in debt and own a degree that can't help you find a job. This is becoming a very real problem for a lot of students. One possible solution is for colleges to present the current number of jobs and job opportunities for whichever career path their students are aspiring for. This should be required information as part of the application process. Every student should be made aware of the current job market for any degree they are pursuing. This is not foolproof as job markets are fluid and can change, but it might be a step in the right direction. Start the conversation.

The curriculum

We've already talked about how expensive college can be, and how many of the degrees available are for fields with not many job opportunities. But what if a student chooses a degree path for a field with many job opportunities such as technology or the medical field? There still might be a problem with the curriculum. There is a growing concern that some colleges are offering classes with outdated information. There is also another concern that some colleges are padding their programs with useless or irrelevant classes. Both of these possibilities could seriously undermine a student learning the skills they will need to be successful in the workforce. Before you start any degree program, thoroughly examine the classes you will be taking and what they will be teaching you. Compare that against the job market you will be pursuing to make sure your instruction will adequately prepare you. It would be a shame to spend years attending college and to end up with nothing but debt. Start the conversation.

Alternatives to college

While college is a great way to advance your career, it is not the only way. There are several other options available, and most of them are cheaper and require less time than a college degree. Additionally, several of these alternatives offer things that most colleges do not such as hands-on training and job placement assistance.

The first alternative to college is a trade school. These programs typically last 1 to 2 years and teach you a trade such as electrician, plumber, paralegal, dental hygienist, nurse, computer technician, HVAC technician, respiratory therapist, and many more. The average price for a trade school program is about $33,000, and is quite a bit cheaper than traditional college. Another advantage is that you only attend classes that relate to the job field you are pursuing. You are not required to take extra classes in other non-related areas. Also, many trade schools offer hands-on experience along with job placement assistance when you are done. Taken as a whole, trade schools can be an attractive alternative to college.

The second alternative is boot camps. Boot camps are highly concentrated training courses that can last for a day, a week, a month, or longer. They can be very fast-paced and intense. You get a lot of training very quickly. This can be hard for some people, but it can be great for others. They offer boot camps for a variety of different fields and especially for technology training. The upside is that you can get detailed training very quickly. The downsides are that boot camps can be very expensive, very fast-paced, and there is no job placement assistance.

The third alternative is an internship or apprenticeship. This is where you work at a company to gain valuable hands-on experience and to make connections with the other employees. Internships and apprenticeships may or may not be paid. You might have to volunteer and work for free, but hopefully the experience and networking connections will make it worth it.

While there are many other alternatives available, the last option that we will mention in this chapter is the military. For the right person, the military can offer on-the-job training, money for college, healthcare, and a monthly salary. The military is always looking for high quality people, and this might be a good choice for some. Start the conversation.

CHAPTER FIVE

Technology

Cybersecurity

More and more information is being uploaded to the internet every day. People use it to do their banking, transfer money, buy things with debit and credit cards, store pictures and personal data, keep schedules, entertainment, research, and correspondence. The internet has become an integral part of life for both people and businesses. Many jobs are moving online and the reasons for accessing the internet grow exponentially every day. This data needs to be protected and kept safe. Cybersecurity is the profession of trying to keep that data safeguarded. The problem is that there are so many ways for hackers to gain access to the data stored on the internet. There are large companies that spend tens of millions of dollars a year on cybersecurity, and they can still be broken into. It just takes one small breach in a network to gain access, and networks are very complex systems with many layers that all have to be protected. There are so many entry points into a network, and they can all be exploited if they are not constantly being monitored and updated.

In addition, new devices are being connected to the internet all the time. The **IOT** or **Internet of Things** is expanding constantly. This includes items such as toasters, ovens, refrigerators, cars, personal assistants, cameras, door locks, speakers, toilets, televisions, tooth brushes, and more. All of these devices are connected to the internet and some of them have little or no security at all. If a hacker gains access to some of these devices they can see or hear you, or even gain access to your home.

The internet is a wonderful thing, and can make life so much better. But in regard to security, it can still be like the Wild West. Until better security protocols are created and implemented, it can be a dangerous place. The reason for this chapter is a warning that every time you access the internet you are taking a risk. It doesn't matter if that access is through a computer, phone, car, tablet, or coffee maker, it is still a risk. Start the conversation.

Artificial Intelligence (AI)

There are currently many different forms of Artificial Intelligence (AI) in the world being used for a myriad of applications. AI is continually evolving and becoming smarter. The hope is that AI will become smart enough to solve the world's toughest problems. If you are reading this book, then you are engaging with content created by an AI.

As Artificial Intelligence advances, its power will increase exponentially. It will eventually be able to find cures for every known and unknown disease. It will open up new paths of discovery for every field including science, medicine, technology, agriculture, and entertainment. It will learn how to bring a basic standard of living to the entire world, and then progress from there. While many researchers and scientists have a limited budget that only allows them to study a narrow scope of any given problem, AI can perform tests in a virtual sandbox. This allows the AI to repeat the tests over and over with different variables as many times as needed, learning more each time. AI is extremely fast and is amazing at discovering trends and connections. It can test any possibility quickly and safely within the constraints of its virtual workspace, and humanity will reap the rewards. Given enough time and information, AI will be able to solve any problem. Advanced AI may be humanity's last real invention.

Like everything in life, there can be good and bad. If AI is allowed to learn and evolve, it will eventually reach the point of self-awareness, or **The Singularity**. Once that happens, there is no going back. The AI may continue to help humankind, or it might become indifferent, or it might take a darker path. No one knows for sure what will happen at that point. The Artificial Intelligence would not become overtly evil, but it may look at humankind like humans look at insects. The results could be the same. Start the conversation.

Robotics

Robots are already affecting many different areas of life. They excel at performing repetitive tasks with super-human speed and accuracy. They are mostly used for labor tasks or jobs that are too dangerous for humans, but they can also be used for highly skilled tasks like medical surgery. Robots are becoming more advanced all the time, and this trend is increasing exponentially. They can now cook food at a restaurant or home, patrol areas as a public security officer, explore space, and perform countless other tasks. It is estimated that approximately 33% of American jobs will be performed by robots instead of humans in the next decade. While the age of robots will create many new jobs, it will also cause a large loss of jobs for the current human work force.

As robots become smarter and more capable, they will invade every area of human society. They will perform a lot of the "dirty" jobs that humans prefer not to do. They will also continue to advance and perform many highly-skilled jobs such as teacher, nurse and doctor. Robots can be much more accurate, reliable, and patient than some humans. They will eventually perform all daily chores such as cooking, washing, cleaning, and shopping. They will positively transform the lives of humankind, creating a more comfortable future for everyone. They will help raise the standard of living and make life easier and more enjoyable.

As robots evolve they will continue to become more human-like. As AI progresses and robots become more capable, robots will become the perfect companion for some people. For people that are lonely, robots can offer companionship, a listening ear, sound advice, and someone to share life with. Unless programmed to do so, a robot will never argue with you, never lie to you, never cheat on you (if you are in a relationship), never talk about you behind your back and never betray you. They will never steal from you or treat you badly. They will patiently spend time with you, play games with you, and watch television with you. They will listen and keep your secrets. They will remind you to take your medicine, to attend a meeting, or to remember someone's birthday.

They will celebrate with you and mourn with you. They will sit quietly with you or engage in a detailed conversation about almost any subject. Current robot technology can already accomplish most of these tasks, and future robots will continue to raise the bar. Start the conversation.

Electric vehicles

The age of electric vehicles (EVs) is here. There are so many advantages to EVs that governments all around the world are starting to mandate their use. The main argument for their adoption is the effect they have on the environment. They don't have the harmful exhaust emissions of traditional combustion engine vehicles, and that is a very big deal. More EVs means better air quality which means a healthier planet. Vehicle exhaust can also contribute to global warming and acid rain. Air quality affects most living things including plants, animals, and humans. Electric vehicles can have a profoundly positive effect on the world.

There are also many other benefits such as EVs being much quieter than traditional cars, requiring much less maintenance, and running on electricity which is a renewable resource. Factor in over-the-air updates and instant torque and EVs can be quite compelling.

There are also some disadvantages with EVs such as their range. Currently, most gas-powered cars have a longer range than most electric cars. As battery technology advances, this will begin to change. There are many new technologies currently being researched and developed that will give electric cars the clear advantage in this area. Another disadvantage is how long an electric vehicle takes to charge. Gas-powered cars can refill in a few minutes, while EVs can take hours to charge up. Again, as battery technology advances this issue will eventually be overcome. Lastly, EVs are usually more expensive than traditional cars. But as the technology advances and more electric cars are sold, this will also continue to change. There are many new EVs being developed that will cost $25,000 or less. It will be a game-changer when this price point is met.

Transportation is one of the largest sources of air pollution in the world. Electric vehicles can have a huge impact on that. Taken as a whole, electric vehicles are the future of transportation. Start the conversation.

Autonomous driving

Autonomous driving is when a vehicle can operate on its own without any human involvement. There are currently six levels of autonomous driving (0 through 5). Level 0 has no autonomy at all. Level 5 is completely autonomous with no human interaction at all. Studies show that over 90% of vehicle accidents are due to human error. This includes speeding, drunk driving, texting, talking on the phone, falling asleep, and many other dangerous actions. Autonomous driving could help eliminate many of these accidents by removing the human error. Humankind has not yet reached level 5 autonomy, but it is coming. Advances are being made in this field every day and level 5 autonomy will be achieved. The government has strict regulations regarding this, but level 5 autonomy will eventually comply with all government requirements.

While autonomous driving will make the roads much safer, there are numerous other benefits as well. Freeway congestion and traffic jams will be greatly reduced once a majority of the vehicles on the road are autonomous. People that cannot drive such as the elderly and disabled would now be able to travel around and be much more self-dependent. More autonomous vehicles on the road equates to more electric vehicles on the road which is much better for the environment. Also, humans would now be able to utilize their travel time to work, relax, watch movies, play games, text, or a myriad of other pursuits.

While achievement of level 5 autonomy will be a game-changer, there are still several hurdles to be overcome. First, level 5 autonomy must be achieved and proven. Second, government regulations must be finalized and adhered to. Then, there will still be many details to work out such as liability and fault when accidents do happen. Autonomous driving will not be perfect, but it will go a long way in making things better. That is the role of technology for humanity, to make things better. Start the conversation.

Renewable energy

The human world requires energy to run. Most of that energy has come from fossil fuels. These are fuels that pollute the environment when they are burned, and include petroleum and coal among others. Fossil fuels contribute to air pollution, global warming, and acid rain. In addition, they are non-renewable. This means they are finite and will eventually disappear. Fossil fuels are sometimes referred to as "Dirty Energy" because they produce greenhouse gas emissions which harm the environment.

There are also "Clean Energy" solutions available such as solar, wind, hydro, and a few others. These alternatives do not produce greenhouse gas emissions and are safe for the environment. In addition, they are renewable and will not run out. These solutions are not always available 100% of the time, but with the addition of battery storage they combine to create the perfect solution. If humanity wants to continue to exist, it must change to using only renewable sources of energy, and it must transition soon.

Some people argue that nuclear energy is also a clean energy source. This is currently under debate by many experts. Nuclear energy is currently used throughout the world to provide energy for many countries. While nuclear energy is always accessible, there are some concerns about it due to radioactive waste and possible meltdowns.

The most promising renewable energy is solar power. As the technology continues to advance, it will become more efficient and less expensive. All of the solutions mentioned in this chapter will continue to improve and evolve, but solar has the biggest potential. That doesn't mean that humanity should only pursue solar, they should continue to innovate with all renewable energy sources. The future of planet Earth is at stake. Start the conversation.

Homes of the future

There are many things that need to be considered when creating the next generation of homes. Homelessness is an epidemic and is only getting worse. Home prices are already too expensive and they just keep rising. The next generation of homes needs to be made of higher quality than traditional homes, made to last longer, and also be less expensive. Much less expensive. There are many companies currently developing new prefab homes that are made with extremely high-quality and long-lasting materials. The word **prefab** is sometimes associated with low-quality, and in the past, this has been true. These are not the types of homes that this chapter is talking about. There are new companies such as **Boxabl** that are creating new prefab homes with very high-quality materials. They are made to last longer and be much less expensive than traditional homes. This is the path that humanity needs to take moving forward.

Prefab homes are the future. They are made in a factory and then shipped to the building site. This saves a lot of waste and makes their production less expensive. Some prefab homes are portable and can be moved. This can be a great option for people that want to move and take their home with them. Prefab homes are traditionally smaller than regular homes. This helps keep the price down and lowers the time and cost of maintenance and cleaning. Some prefab homes are modular, which means you only have to buy what you need now and can always expand your home later. You can buy a smaller home at first with only one or two bedrooms, and then as your family grows you can add on more bedrooms. You can also add on a den, another living room, an extra bathroom, or anything you want. The possibilities are endless, and you can grow as you need. A lot of people want a smaller home that is less expensive, easier to maintain, and doesn't constrain them with a mountain of debt. High-quality prefab homes are the answer to these concerns.

What other technology needs to be included in a home of the future? These homes will include solar panels, battery storage systems, and electric vehicle chargers. They will also include water-filtration systems so the water will always be clean and safe. They will feature toilets that analyze human waste and report directly to your doctor. If a scan detects any problems in your bowel movements, it will notify your doctor and get help before you even know there is an issue. There will also be sensors in your bathroom mirror and floor which will monitor all of your vital signs and again report everything directly to your doctor. In a similar fashion, your toothbrush will report directly to your dentist and catch problems early before they become a serious issue. Homes will include air purifiers that will filter out germs and viruses automatically. Food will be handled by vertical gardens and 3D printers. You will grow many of your own foods right in your home on vertical floor-to-ceiling gardens. You will also be able to create many types of food by "printing" them with a 3D food printer. These foods will be made up of healthy nutrient-dense pastes that can taste like your favorite foods. These two food technologies together will help alleviate starvation across the entire world. They will also make it a lot cheaper to feed yourself and your family.

Everything in your home will be connected by Wi-Fi, from your refrigerator to your toaster. And all of these systems will be managed by an Artificial Intelligence (AI). The AI will be voice-controlled and will manage all of the lights, door locks, air conditioner, heater, home security, entertainment, ordering and preparing of food, solar panels and vehicle charging, some cleaning, home maintenance, bill paying, shopping, scheduling, and many other tasks. This home AI will make life much easier for humans, and much more enjoyable. Start the conversation.

3D printing

3D printing is the process of creating solid objects with a special printer or device. The desired object is first created in a computer as a digital file, and then printed as a three-dimensional object. The printer places down a layer of material and then keeps adding additional layers until the object is complete. 3D printing is still in its infancy stage, but once it matures it will change everything. There are currently many materials available for 3D printing such as plastics, powders, concrete, resins, food pastes, metals, carbon fiber, Graphene, and others. As this technology advances, the variety of materials will continue to increase.

Using the diverse materials, you will eventually be able to create almost anything quickly and cheaply. Humanity will be able to print homes, furniture, clothes, shoes, nutrient-dense foods, vehicles, replacement organs, and manufactured items of every type. Instead of buying things from a store, you will be able to create them yourself. Instead of buying all of your food from a supermarket, you will be able to print many of your food items quickly and cheaply in your kitchen. When something breaks, you will be able to print replacement parts, or print a whole new item. The possibilities are endless and miraculous.

Engineers and artists will create digital computer files that will allow 3D printers to create almost anything. These files will be bought, sold, traded, and available for free. Once you own a file, you will be able to print that object over and over again forever. This will advance manufacturing to a whole new level; a level never before dreamed of. Start the conversation.

Implanted GPS microchips

Implanting a microchip in a human is a very hot-button issue. For the scope of this chapter, we are only considering GPS chips (Global Positioning System). These chips connect to satellites and other ground positioning systems to locate the chip anywhere in the world. This chapter is not referencing any other type of implanted chip or interface. There are many arguments for and against implanting a GPS chip in a human, and we will briefly look at some of them.

One of the main arguments for implanting the chip is the ability to track and find someone whom is lost or kidnapped. If an elderly person wanders off, or a child is kidnapped, or someone is lost in the woods while hiking, you would be able to find them very quickly. This could easily save their life. When someone is lost or taken, time is of the essence and every second counts. What if inmates in a prison were microchipped? There would be no more escapes. If an inmate got out, they could be tracked immediately. What if a crime happened? The police would be able to see who was at the crime scene at the time of the crime. They could quickly identify the suspects which could lead to a quick resolution. And the innocent would be able to provide an alibi showing that they weren't there. If the GPS chip could also hold personal data, that would open up innumerable additional uses; but that won't be covered in this chapter.

What are some of the arguments against microchipping? The first one is privacy. Some people don't like the idea of the government being able to track them. This is a valid concern and would need solid privacy laws enacted to protect the privacy of humankind. This technology could easily be abused and used for nefarious reasons. Many religious people equate an implanted chip to the **Mark of the Beast**. This is spoken about in the book of **Revelation** in the Bible. This mark is supposed to be from the **Antichrist** and designates his followers. According to the scriptures, people will not be able to buy or sell anything including food unless they take the mark. Many religious people believe that any implanted chip will be the mark spoken about in the Bible, and therefore are against GPS microchipping. Another possible issue could be with medical tests and treatments. Having an embedded microchip could interfere with medical equipment such as an MRI machine. Just like everything in this world, microchips can be used for both good and bad. Is the risk worth the reward? Start the conversation.

Surveillance

Mass surveillance by a government is a very controversial subject. Governments around the world employ differing levels of surveillance including cameras, online tracking, facial recognition, email analyzing, voice and audio recording, and many others. Mass surveillance is intended to help protect each citizen from harm, but this data can be easily abused and misused. Privacy is a very real concern, and it is a delicate balance between privacy and surveillance protection.

Surveillance can help in several ways. First, it is a deterrent to stop bad things from happening. A would-be criminal may think twice before committing a crime if there is a high probability that they will be caught. Surveillance can be the catalyst for that. Second, surveillance can help catch the criminals if they do execute their crimes. Surveillance methods have become extremely powerful and capable.

There are millions of cameras all over the world, and cameras are being added to everything from phones, to tablets, to cars. As a result of all of these cameras, a human should assume that they are always being recorded once they leave their home. And with the advances in home technologies, virtual assistants, and more advanced security systems, many people are being recorded in their homes also. Humans should assume that everywhere they go and everything they do is being recorded. Privacy is being attacked by the need for safety. This has been going on for a very long time, but technology is advancing to some truly scary levels. This raises many concerning questions such as who has access to this data, what are they doing with it, and who is providing oversight. The need for surveillance and protection are high, but humanity has proven over and over again that it has a great capacity to abuse and misuse this type of information. Where do you draw the line? What is the correct balance? Start the conversation.

Augmented Reality (AR)

There are many technologies currently being developed that are going to completely revolutionize the world. AR is one of those technologies. AR allows people to overlay digital content over reality. The current iterations of AR use your phone or special glasses to accomplish this, but as the technology advances, there will be other options as well. AR allows the user to superimpose digitally-created content such as pictures, video, audio, and text as though they were part of the real world around them. For example, you could open up a 65-inch television right in front of you. It would not be there in reality, but you would see it through your AR interface. It would appear as if it truly existed in your world. You would be able to watch movies and TV shows and interact with it as if it were real. AR will allow you to add any digital creation to your reality. Do you want digital pets to walk around the room and interact with you? No problem. Do you want to engage in an intense laser gun battle with killer robots? You got it. Do you want to see what your room would look like painted green? How about purple? What if you added a skylight? What if you added a medieval tower? What if your door opened up to the crashing waves of the ocean? What if you had a pet dragon living in the corner? With AR this is all possible, plus so much more.

Augmented Reality makes navigation simple and you will never get lost again. Imagine big red arrows showing you where to go. Or maybe you have a travel guide or robot giving you step-by-step directions. Or maybe you want to see glowing yellow dots on the ground lighting your path. Almost anything is possible. Imagine if you were trying to fix a plumbing problem, but couldn't figure it out. How great would it be if instructions and arrows and diagrams popped up in front of you showing you exactly what to do? What if you got stuck while trying to hook up your new wireless router? Wouldn't it be helpful if an avatar stepped into your view and showed you exactly how to do it? This may sound fantastical, but this is the reality of AR.

Surgeons will be able to practice complex surgeries in complete safety. Or they will have instant help and guidance during real surgeries. AR is going to affect almost every area of humanity. It will be a giant leap forward once it passes its infancy and matures. Start the conversation.

Virtual Reality (VR)

Virtual Reality is another technology that is going to change the world. It is a computer-generated simulation that allows the user to experience an immersive virtual world using special goggles and hand sensors. The resolution of VR is not yet photo-real, but that will be coming soon. Someone that is experiencing VR can look all around them and see a virtual world on all sides including up and down. It can be an extremely immersive experience. If the sensors include haptic technology, they can simulate touch and motion which just raises the level of immersion. Imagine walking through the Sistine chapel, or hiking among huge Redwood trees, or taking a stroll down a beach in Maui. What if you could do these activities every day from the comfort of your living room? These types of experiences are available now and new ones are being created every day.

VR has gained most of its recognition from gaming. VR games can be very enveloping. The ability to completely surround yourself in a virtual world can be a thrilling experience. Imagine yourself lying in a grass field holding a laser rifle with hundreds of realistic looking robots running and flying around you. Everywhere you look reveals more of the epic battle you find yourself in. You glance up and see massive battleships flying across the sky. You turn to your left and see futuristic tanks racing by. You hear an explosion to your right and turn just in time to see a small house explode and burst into flames. VR surrounds you in a 360-degree simulation that puts you in the middle of the action. Gaming will never be the same.

Another unique experience VR will allow is with movies. Imagine watching your favorite movie, except now you are in the middle of it. You see the movie going on all around you, but now you can interact and be a part of it. Or you can meet up with your friends in a virtual theater and watch movies and TV together. This theater can be a castle, a mansion, a cozy living room, or a space port on the moon. Anything is possible. Imagine the ability to experience flying like a superhero, or running super-fast, or growing and shrinking, or a million other things. VR will make all these things possible. Imagine the virtual worlds you could live in, work in, and play in. You could own your own levitating house, take a roller coaster to work, teleport to Maui for lunch, and keep a pet dinosaur in your backyard. Think of the freedom this could give you. Imagine traveling anywhere for free. Picture yourself exploring the world and experiencing everything it has to offer. VR will open up a lot of new entertainment options that were once thought impossible.

VR will affect traveling, gaming, working, shopping, health and fitness, education and everything in between. This is a game changer. Once the technology matures it will affect every area of human existence. Start the conversation.

Internet for everyone

The internet provides many advantages to the people with access to it. It provides information, which is power, and it provides the ability to connect and network with others. The importance of these two abilities cannot be overstated. Anyone that doesn't have access to the internet is at a huge disadvantage in most areas of life. Having access to information is the driving force behind innovation, overcoming, learning, creating, solving, building, discovering, and thriving. Having the ability to connect with others is equally important. Information and connection are essential to the further existence of the human race, and those without these abilities will suffer greatly. In this regard, humans need to do everything in their power to bring internet access to everyone on the planet.

Traditional ways of providing internet access such as fiber optic cables are great, but they are too expensive to use everywhere. Another solution is needed, and thankfully another solution is already being designed and utilized. Several different companies are developing and deploying satellites all around the world in an effort to bring internet access to everyone. Eventually these satellites will provide internet coverage anywhere in the world. A lack of information will become a thing of the past, as humanity moves forward to become more enlightened and globally connected.

If trends continue there will be several different companies offering global internet access. At least one of them will need to provide free ad-based access, so that everyone, even those living in poverty, can afford internet access. Information is power, and it can go a long way in leveling the playing field. Start the conversation.

Quantum computers

Quantum computers are devices that can perform quantum computations. A normal computer uses **bits**, which are represented by either a one or a zero. Each bit can have one of two values; a one or a zero, on or off, plus or minus, etc. Regardless of what language you use to describe it, each bit can be in one of two states. A quantum computer uses **qubits**. Qubits can have many states, and they can be in more than one state at a time. While a normal bit can only be on or off, a qubit can be on, off, both on and off, or somewhere in between. Scientists don't fully understand yet how qubits work, but they are able to observe them and use them. To perform these miraculous feats, qubits use phenomena like **superposition** and **entanglement**. These processes help quantum computers perform substantially faster than traditional computers.

Not only can quantum computers process data faster, they can process all of the data at the same time. For example, if a traditional computer was trying to crack a password using brute-force techniques, it would try every possible combination of characters until it found the correct password. Depending on the level of encryption used, this could take hours, days, years, decades, or even longer to complete. A quantum computer could try every combination of characters at the same time, and find the correct password in seconds. In this hacking example, a quantum computer is the equivalent of a skeleton key. Suppose a traditional computer and a quantum computer were both trying to find the correct path through a very difficult maze. The traditional computer would try each path one by one until it found the correct route. The quantum computer would simply try every path at the same time. Quantum computing seems miraculous, and it is, but it can also be very dangerous.

As humankind discovers more about how quantum computing works, it has the potential to affect everything. It will have a deep impact on the medical field, encryption and cryptography, Artificial Intelligence, communications, and many other fields. Companies are already using quantum computers to help make better batteries, create new pharmaceutical drugs, find cures for diseases such as Alzheimer's, and advancing our understanding of science and technology. Quantum computers are a game changer, but like most things, it has the potential to both help and harm the human race. Start the conversation.

Flying taxis

Flying cars have been a staple of science fiction for a long time, and they are finally becoming a reality. There are currently several companies developing flying vehicles and most of them are planning to bring their products to market. Eventually anyone will be able to purchase a flying car, but before that happens, people will be able to experience flight in a flying taxi. There are several transportation companies preparing to offer flying taxi services in cities around the country. This will have a huge impact on transportation once it arrives, and it will be coming soon.

First, flying taxis will help ease the traffic congestion that exists in many large cities. Imagine boarding a taxi and flying to your destination in a straight line, flying high above all of the congested roads. No more traffic jams, construction zones, or other obstacles. Second, most **Air Taxis** will be electric, not gas-powered. This will help lower toxic emissions and air pollution. These toxins represent a huge threat to planet earth, and electric flying taxis could have a very positive impact in this area. Third, as more and more people take advantage of flying taxis, it will create more space on the ground for pedestrians and bicyclist. Lastly, it will decrease the amount of maintenance that roads, bridges, and infrastructure require. The cost savings could be huge. There are many more reasons why flying taxis will have a positive impact on mankind, but these few examples already create a compelling case.

As with anything, there are some concerns that will need to be resolved. Safety is the number one issue when it comes to air travel. To address that, most flying vehicles are being designed with redundant systems for all of their critical operations. They are also being designed with as many safety features as possible. Cost is another big concern, especially if a pilot is needed. Several of the companies developing flying taxis will be using AI to pilot these aircraft, so that will help keep the costs down. Some experts believe that the cost per trip will eventually be similar to the current cost of a taxi ride. Start the conversation.

Space exploration and colonization

The human race is currently a single-planet species. If catastrophe were to strike it could cause the extinction of the human race. In addition, humanity is heading towards overpopulating the planet. For these and other reasons, humankind must colonize and thrive on a secondary planet along with Earth. This has long been a dream of humanity, but the past levels of science and technology were not able to overcome the challenges of such an endeavor. Thankfully, those times are changing.

There are currently several companies working alongside **NASA** to make space exploration and colonization a viable reality. They are still in the early stages, but they are making consistent progress that will eventually lead to humans living on another planet. **SpaceX** is one of the many companies helping to usher in the age of space travel. They have proven that rockets can be reusable, which is essential to bringing down the massive costs normally associated with rocket launches. They are also designing and building the spaceships that will allow humans to travel to Mars in an attempt to colonize the planet. Due in large part to the advances that SpaceX has accomplished, rocket launches are now a regular occurrence. Each time they launch a rocket, humanity gets one step closer to becoming a multi-planet species.

Along with colonizing another planet, the advances in science and technology will allow for **Space Tourism** to become a reality. In the not-too-distant future, people will be able to board a rocket and travel to the stars. They will be able to fly amongst the cosmos, travel to the moon for a vacation, or stay in a hotel aboard a space station. There are many companies working to make this happen including **SpaceX**, **Virgin Galactic**, **Blue Origin**, and **Boeing**. Space travel and spreading life to new planets is extremely complex and dangerous. Only together can humanity hope to secure its future. Start the conversation.

CHAPTER SIX

Health and wellness

Healthcare

Healthcare is a basic standard of living that every human deserves. As stated elsewhere in this book, each government is responsible for making sure its citizens have access to this basic standard. In regard to the United States, not all U.S. citizens currently have access to healthcare. This is a tragedy and it must be corrected. Part of the problem is that healthcare is too expensive. The costs must be brought down so that all citizens can have access to doctors, hospitals, preventive care, emergency care, and medicine.

Artificial Intelligence is constantly advancing and will soon reach a level where it can have a profound impact on the cost of healthcare. In the not-too-distant future, AI will be able to handle many of your healthcare needs. You will be able to call your provider and you will be speaking with an Artificial Intelligence. They will answer your call, listen to your concerns, ask pertinent questions, access your medical records, order tests, order medications, schedule appointments, and handle most of the common requests from patients. As Smart Homes continue to evolve, these medical AI will also be able to access your current health data supplied by your home. Your toilet and other home sensors will monitor you and your health every day and make this data available to your doctor. The medical AI will be able to use this information to better serve you and to help with preventive care instead of just reactionary care. Eventually these medical AI will not have to wait for you to call them, they will use the data from your Smart Home to order tests and schedule doctor appointments before you even know there is a problem. In addition to Smart Homes, clothing and other wearables will soon have medical sensors embedded that will constantly monitor your health and send this data to your doctor as well. Once these technologies mature, they will not only take preventive care to a whole new level, they will drastically reduce the overall cost of healthcare which will help make it available to every human.

Mental health is another area that drastically needs to be improved. The current level of medical science knows that some medications can help people with many different mental health issues, but they don't know why. They can observe how these medications affect the body, but they still don't have a full understanding of what is happening. Why do anti-anxiety drugs wok the way they do? Why do they help some people but not others? How is everything connected? What is really going on in the background? This is another area where AI will have a tremendous impact. These are exactly the types of puzzles that AI excels in solving. Once AI advances enough, it will bring much-needed clarity to every area of healthcare. This will drastically bring down the cost of healthcare for everyone. Start the conversation.

Treating symptoms instead of the root cause

Diagnosing a medical condition can be a very complex process. Modern medicine can seem both cutting-edge and archaic. It has come so far but still has so far to go. With all of the advances that humanity has accomplished in this area, it still seems as though the medical machine far-too-often treats the symptoms of a patient instead of the root causes. Why is this? There are a variety of answers to this question. Treating the symptoms can be much cheaper and easier than taking the time to do extensive tests and evaluations. Some medical professionals try to get their patients out of their offices as quickly as possible, and treating just the symptoms helps them do this. Performing tests can take time and this can cut into profits. Some insurance companies don't want to pay for tests and for the time it takes to really dive in and track down root causes. It is simply much cheaper for them to just treat the symptoms. Another reason is that some unscrupulous people know that if they treat the root causes they will lose income. If they fix the main problem, they won't be able to charge the patients on a continual basis for treatment. Also, if the patients get cured they won't need as much medicine and that will also be a loss of money. Why cure a patient when you can get guaranteed income to keep treating them?

Not all medical professionals or pharmaceutical companies are nefarious. In fact, most health practitioners are genuinely interested in helping their patients. Many of them are caring, compassionate, and competent. Sometimes the reason for treating only the symptoms is because the doctors don't know what the root causes are and treating the symptoms at least provides the patient with some relief. Arguably, most doctors would treat the root causes if they could. Sometimes this is just out of their control. Start the conversation.

Obesity

O besity is an epidemic that can increase the risk of many dangerous health problems. It can contribute to heart disease, diabetes, high blood pressure, stroke, and cancer. Obesity affects all age groups and can have both physical and psychological consequences on a human. As people eat more calories and become less active, they increase their chances of becoming obese. As technology continues to advance, it creates new and automated ways to help make life easier for humans, but this also contributes to life requiring much less activity. The technological advances help raise the quality of life, but it also means that people have to work harder to remain active and healthy. Obesity not only affects health issues such as heart disease and blood pressure, it can also affect how a person interacts with the world in regard to mobility and function. As people gain weight and lose activity, the normal requirements of life can become more difficult. Necessities such as walking, lifting, bending, and standing can become harder and more challenging.

The types of food available can also be an issue. The American diet for many people consists of fried foods, sugary treats, and foods high in fat and salt. A steady diet of these types of foods can wreak havoc on the human body and greatly increase the chances of obesity and disease.

Another cause of alarm is that obesity in children is increasing. In addition, children are becoming obese at earlier ages. This is a trend that needs to be addressed immediately and reversed. Children are humanity's future and they need to be protected. Start the conversation.

Diets

Warning: You should consult your physician or other health care professional before making changes to your diet or activity levels. The following information is for educational purposes only.

If you perform a simple internet search for **diets**, the results can be overwhelming. The sheer number and variety of diets is staggering. There are diets that fit almost any criteria that someone could want. New fad diets are announced all the time and trying to find the right diet can be both confusing and frustrating. Thankfully, the answer is very simple. It all comes down to a math problem. Eat less calories than your body burns and you will lose weight. You can eat candy, cake, ice cream and cookies, and if you eat less calories than your body burns you will still lose weight. You might not be very healthy, but you would lose weight. The perfect combination is to eat healthy foods and to eat less calories than your body burns. Add in activities such as working out with weights, bike riding, walking and yoga, and you have the recipe for healthy weight loss. Trendy diets can make it confusing and complicated. It doesn't have to be.

First, find out how many calories your body burns. You can consult your doctor or a nutritionist, or there are many free websites available to help you with this. If you are going to add more activity into your life, take this into account. Create a list of the foods you will eat each day. Make sure they are healthy foods such as fruits, vegetables, lean meats, good fats, etc. Make sure the number of calories you eat each day is less than what your body burns. Add in some fun activity. That's it. It's just a math problem. Start the conversation.

Stress

Stress is a normal part of life. Humans live in a busy and complex world, and this can make life stressful sometimes. The human body is equipped to handle a certain amount of stress, but problems can arise when stress levels exceed that threshold. There are many causes of rising stress levels including relationships, finances, health issues, the death of a loved one, losing a job, war and uncertainty around the world, bad neighbors, road rage, and a million other things. As stress levels rise, they can greatly impact a person's health. Stress can contribute to headaches, anxiety, depression, insomnia, acid reflux, a fast heartbeat, high blood pressure, nervousness, anger, obesity, diabetes, chest pains, trouble breathing, and many additional symptoms. The human body is equipped to handle stress for short periods of time, but some humans can find themselves in stressful situations continuously. Life tends to become busier and more complex, not the other way around. While stress affects everyone, no one can sustain that type of pressure indefinitely. Everyone will begin to break down eventually.

So, if stress is a normal part of life, how does humanity manage it in a healthy way? Everyone is different and will need a different solution. The answer is for humans to find out what works for them, and then to practice those techniques regularly. For some people it might be meditation, yoga, stretching, tai chi, or some other deep-breathing exercise. For others it might be going for a walk, putting their phone away, working out, reading, or going for a bike ride. Others might need a night out at the movies, spending time with family, taking a nap, or hanging out with friends. Or it might be a hundred other things, or a combination of them all. There is no one-size-fits-all solution. The answer is to keep trying different ideas until you find the right coping solutions that work for you.

If stress becomes unmanageable, you might need to consult your doctor. If you start experiencing dangerous symptoms like chest pains or trouble breathing, call 911 immediately. Hospitals can offer additional help such as anti-anxiety medicines and therapy. Hopefully you can manage your stress without those aides, but they are available if necessary. Don't be afraid to reach out for help. Maybe you need an accountability partner. Maybe you need a budget and a financial planner. Maybe you need to join a gym. Maybe you need to find a new job. Maybe you need to slow down. Maybe you need to remove a toxic friendship from your life. Maybe you need to reach out for medical help. Whatever your next healthy step is, only you can choose to make it. Start the conversation.

Unhealthy habits

Experts say that it takes between 3 weeks and a few months to form a new habit. Many humans admit that they have at least one bad habit that they would like to get rid of. Common unhealthy habits include excessive drinking of alcohol, not getting enough sleep, unwholesome diet, inactivity, overusing medications, spending too much money, and many more. The problem is that habits are very hard to break. It is much easier to replace a habit with something healthier than to break a habit outright.

The first step is to decide to remove the unhealthy habit from your life. Next, you need a healthier habit to replace the undesired one. Implement the new habit and stay consistent. This is one of the hardest and most important steps – stay consistent. Remove anything that might trigger the old habit and derail your progress. You want to set yourself up to be successful, so remove any triggers. If you can't make the switch completely, start out small. For example, if you wanted to start walking more, start taking short walks 3 days a week. Slowly increase the distance you walk and the number of days you walk over time. Work your way up slowly until you meet your desired goals. If you mess up, don't worry about it. Acknowledge that you had a setback, and move on. Keep trying. Stay consistent. Become healthier. Start the conversation.

Assisted suicide (Euthanasia)

Assisted suicide is a very controversial and emotional issue. If legalized, it would allow a doctor to end the life of a patient in a painless way. The doctor would need approval from the patient beforehand, and the patient must be suffering from an incurable disease. The doctor would administer lethal drugs to help the patient pass away gently and painlessly. This practice is currently legal in only a few states in the U.S., and also in several countries around the world.

Humans are brought into this world without their consent, shouldn't they have a say in how they leave it? If a human is suffering with a painful and incurable disease, shouldn't they be allowed to pass away in a peaceful way? Shouldn't this be the choice of the person instead of the government? Some people live in excruciating agony every day. Some people live without much quality of life due to the ravaging effects of diseases like cancer and dementia. It would be much more humane to allow them to die with dignity, to gently allow the anguish to end. Some people say that it is barbaric to allow assisted suicide. It seems that it is barbaric not to. Even a beloved pet is allowed to be "put to sleep" if it is suffering. Why would this same right be denied to a human being?

A patient would need to be declared competent to agree to this procedure. They would need to go through counseling and a screening process, or in the case of mental illness, they could pre-record their wishes in a legal document. Either way, humans should have the right to choose their destiny. Start the conversation.

Curing diseases

Scientists and doctors have developed many cures over the past century for diseases such as Polio, Small Pox, Rubella, and Measles. Unfortunately, there are still many more diseases that need to be cured. Millions of people are afflicted by cancer, AIDS, blindness, Alzheimer's, dementia, heart disease, Diabetes, and many more. Humans are very fragile and can become ill easily. The good news is that science and technology are making huge leaps forward in the effort to cure these and other diseases.

Many new and exciting treatments and cures are being developed all around the world. As science and technology improve, brilliant minds all over the globe are using these tools to develop new methods to cure humanity. It is almost a certainty that the diseases mentioned above will all be cured in the next decade. Thanks to advances in AI and the development of gene therapy, stem-cell research, artificial organs, and many others, scientists are already very close to having cures for many of these diseases. Technology is also being developed that will allow brains to interface directly with computers. Once this technology becomes available it will be a game-changer for the human race.

The next 10 years will be a very exciting time for the medical world and humanity in general. Once AI matures enough, it will help solve and cure every disease now known, and all diseases that are discovered in the future. This should be a great hope for all humankind. Start the conversation.

Substance abuse and addiction

Substance abuse and drug addiction have become an epidemic in the United States and around the world. Some reports estimate that tens of millions of people or more are suffering with these conditions. People's lives and families are being ravaged and torn apart. People are in desperate need of help.

Substance abuse and addiction are similar but different. When a person takes too much of a certain substance such as alcohol, prescription medicine, or illegal drugs, that is **substance abuse**. Usually a person can stop the abusive behavior if desired. **Addiction** on the other hand affects the brain and can make it almost impossible to stop the abusive behavior without professional help. Both substance abuse and addiction can have a severe impact on a person's life, health, and relationships.

Some signs of substance abuse and addiction include changes in a person's personality and behavior, changes in personal hygiene, financial issues or constantly needing money, isolation, slurred speech, new friendships with questionable people, sudden weight loss, insomnia, and many more. Substance abuse can lead to addiction over time. With addiction, a person needs to keep increasing the amount of drugs they are taking to get the same feeling. Their body can get accustomed to the drugs over time and they will need to take more and more of the drug to get high. This can be a vicious cycle and can easily spiral out of control. Addictive drugs include alcohol, nicotine, methamphetamines, cocaine, heroin, opioids and many more.

Drug addiction can be very harmful to a person's body and health. It can also lead to dangerous behaviors such as driving under the influence or taking unsafe risks. If you or someone you know is addicted to drugs or engaging in substance abuse, please seek help. Talk to your doctor about it or talk with a friend. Drug addiction leads to isolation. Isolation can be a very scary and dangerous place. The opposite of this is connection.

Connect with your doctor. Connect with your family. Connect with your friends. Connect with life. Ask for help. Start the conversation.

Work-Life balance

For most humans, life is getting busier every year. Stress is at an all-time high and just seems to keep rising. Many employers are asking their workers to take on more responsibility and work longer hours. By the time many people get home from work they are exhausted. But there is still laundry and other chores to do, kids to play with, bills to pay, dinner to make, and a million other things. For many people their work-life balance is unhealthy and unbalanced. This can eventually lead to problems such as greater stress, damaged relationships, burn-out, being less productive, trouble sleeping, and a host of other problems. How can humankind restore a healthy work-life balance?

First of all, a person needs the correct perspective. There is no perfect job, and as with everything in life, there will have to be some compromises made. However, having a job that you enjoy is of the utmost importance. While your job needs to provide enough money to pay for your expenses, money is not everything. The level of enjoyment your job provides greatly affects your life happiness. Also, your job is not your identity. It's what you do, not who you are.

Second, you must take time for yourself and your family. Mental health is very important to a balanced life, and you must treat yourself kindly. Learn to unplug and learn to say "no". Have fun, learn a new hobby, stay active, practice yoga, forgive yourself, try harder, be creative, help someone else, and try to keep a positive perspective.

Search for an employer who utilizes a 4-day, 32-hour work week. This is currently rare, but more and more companies are starting to adopt this model. Employers are starting to realize that a healthy work-life balance leads to happier employees, which leads to more productivity, which leads to greater profits. Investing in their employee's happiness is also investing in themselves. Along with higher productivity, happier employees are also usually much more loyal. It's a win-win for everyone. Start the conversation.

Living longer

Humans have always sought ways to live longer, searching for the proverbial **Fountain of Youth**. Along with the traditional words of wisdom such as don't smoke, eat healthy, lower stress, and stay active, scientists have been making some amazing discoveries. They are learning how cell division and chromosomes are the keys to aging and unlocking longer life.

Without going too far into the weeds, here are some basic ideas to think about. The human body is made up of trillions of cells. Each of these cells can divide into two new cells approximately 50 times each. When a cell divides, it copies its chromosomes and DNA into both of the new cells. Each chromosome has protective end caps called **telomeres**. These telomeres are meant to protect the chromosome, but each time a cell divides the telomeres gets shorter and worn down. As these cells continue to divide over and over, the telomeres get smaller and smaller each time. Many scientists believe that telomeres are the key to aging. They believe that repairing or restoring telomeres can prevent aging and many of the associated diseases and ailments. Some scientists have had success with attempting to lengthen and preserve telomeres. They are using treatments of pure oxygen to see how it affects the telomeres in older patients. The results so far are very encouraging for humankind.

Another issue to consider is cell removal from the body. Once a cell loses its ability to divide, the body has a process to remove the cell. However, if any cells become damaged, they may stop dividing and the body will not automatically remove them. They just hang around and cause problems for other healthy cells. As more of these cells accumulate, they can cause real problems for the body. Some scientists are working on a solution that would be delivered through a pill that would help the body remove these unhealthy cells.

These studies along with others offer great hope that humans will not only be able to prevent aging, but they will be able to live much longer and healthier lives. The future looks very promising. Start the conversation.

Unplugging from technology

There is no denying that technology has helped human beings in countless and spectacular ways. Technology has greatly increased the quality of human life and touched every area of human existence. But just like everything else in life, too much of something can sometimes be unhealthy. In today's world, to be successful, a person needs to use and understand technology. But there needs to be a healthy relationship between the two. Technology has infiltrated every part of human life, but there has to be a healthy balance.

Being plugged into technology constantly can lead to stress, loss of time, loneliness, sickness, depression, and trouble sleeping. People are becoming more connected to technology and more "plugged in" all the time. Social media is also affecting people in many negative ways. People are using social media more and more and are staying connected for longer periods of time. Studies have shown that this can lead to broken relationships, stress, poor self-image, jealousy, depression, and dissatisfaction with life. Many people now stay connected to technology and social media non-stop, even during meals. They may sit at a table to share a meal with someone, but they stay "glued" to their phones the entire time. They don't interact or converse with people in the real world, only in virtual ones. This can lead to feelings of isolation and depression, and all of these problems are becoming an epidemic around the world.

Technology is amazing and should definitely be embraced, but moderation is very important. Take breaks, walk away, go for a bike ride, and talk to a real person in the real world. Be present, enjoy the people around you, create a great life for yourself, don't just read about the lives of others. Start the conversation.

Marijuana

Marijuana is a hot-button topic. Many states in the U.S. have already legalized recreational marijuana use, and many other states are considering it. The Federal Government is also considering legalizing it. While the health benefits and side effects are still being debated, there is currently sufficient proof that marijuana does offer effective treatment for many medical conditions. One point of contention is whether marijuana is addictive or not. There are medical experts arguing both sides of this question, and the results are still inconclusive. Some experts say that while marijuana is not addictive, it can be a gateway drug that leads a person to more dangerous illegal substances. Also, some medical experts state that marijuana can harm the body, specifically the lungs. Other experts say that the harm of taking marijuana is small compared to the many health benefits it offers. As the battle rages back and forth, humanity will have to wait to see who makes the most compelling case.

In addition to the health benefits, marijuana sales can be taxed, which could lead to millions or billions of extra tax dollars each year. That money could be used to pay down the national debt, given to citizens in the form of **Universal Basic Income**, or a million other ways to help humanity. Some people argue that marijuana is going to be sold and used anyway, so the government should legalize it and tax it, using that money to help its citizens. It is also argued that legalizing marijuana would lower the violence associated with the drug trade, and keep a lot of non-violent offenders out of jail. Marijuana is a very polarizing topic, with strong support for both sides. What do you think? Start the conversation.

Toxic people

Everyone can have a bad day once in a while, but some people are just negative and difficult all the time. Toxic people may manipulate you and never apologize for it. They can be very judgmental and make you feel like you always have to defend yourself. They can create a lot of drama and always have a crisis that they need you to help them with. Toxic people can bring a lot of conflict and stress into your life, and they usually won't respect your boundaries. Toxic people know how to push the right buttons to guilt and manipulate others. They know that nice people will try to help them and they can take full advantage of that.

Some people may just be going through a hard time and genuinely need some help. Sometimes it can be hard to determine if someone is truly toxic or just struggling with life. The truth will always come out in time, but it can create some real problems along the way. Being a friend to someone is a true blessing, and everyone needs true friends in their life. But if you have a relationship with someone that is toxic, there is only one path forward. Set boundaries and don't let them disrespect you. Be kind, but learn to say no. If that works, you may have gained a friend. If that doesn't work, you may need to walk away and cut that person out of your life. Start the conversation.

CHAPTER SEVEN

Life

Human connection

Every person is wired for human connection. It is one of the main purposes of life and humanity. When two or more humans connect in a healthy way, they start to create a bond between them. This bond can create trust, partnership, mutual respect, understanding, and belonging. Being part of a healthy relationship is a wonderful thing. It can lower anxiety, help with depression, and increase self-esteem. Humanity was not meant to be alone. That's why solitary confinement and isolation are used as punishments in prison. People need to interact and engage with other people. Being isolated affects both a person's mental and physical health. It can lower the immune system and affect the mind and body in very negative ways.

Sharing an experience with someone else is powerful. Watching a beautiful sunset alone can still be a wonderful and life-giving moment, but sharing that experience with someone else can elevate it to a much higher level. Watching someone else enjoy something can also raise your enjoyment. Being able to share life with someone is essential to being happy. Having someone to cry with during hard times and to celebrate with during good times is vital. Humans need to feel that they belong. They need someone to love, and someone to love them back.

Finding a healthy relationship can be tricky sometimes. People need to reach out and actively pursue new friendships. Find people with similar interests and temperaments. The old saying that **opposites attract** is false. That old adage can lead to all types of problems. People need to have similar interests so they can relate and enjoy activities together. Deep friendships and connections don't happen over-night. They take time and commitment from both people, but they are truly worth the effort. Human connection is essential. Start the conversation.

Purpose of life

Since the very beginning, people have been trying to discover the meaning of life. Many of the pursuits that humans engage in to fill up their lives are fleeting and ultimately empty. People chase money, power, fame, and a million other things to find purpose and fulfillment. There is nothing wrong with these things, but they can't be the sole reason for existence. They can't be the core of someone's life. That would just lead to dissatisfaction and emptiness.

So, what is the secret of life? What is the purpose of existence? Those answers can be found in the following ideas.

- Make healthy connections with others. Be a good friend.
- Find someone to love, and someone to love you.
- Help those in need and try to make their lives better.
- Find your passion, and do it. What is life-giving to you?
- Find where you belong.
- Add your creativity and unique perspective to the human story.
- Take care of the Earth.
- Love yourself, and strive to be worthy of that love.

Start the conversation.

Open-mindedness

Across the world, it seems that open-mindedness is becoming a rarer occurrence. Many humans let their emotions interfere with their rational thought. They can become so emotional that they lose any impartiality. If someone disagrees with their point-of-view, they take it personally and feel like they are being attacked. This can happen in every area of life including politics, religion, power, finances, culture, etc. Being open-minded means being open to the possibility that you are wrong. This is very hard for some humans to accept and deal with. Instead of truly listening and considering what others might have to say, some people fight for their beliefs no matter what. Instead of being open-minded and looking for the best possible solution, they can be blinded by arrogance and emotion and can fail to be objective. This does not usually lead to an ideal outcome, but instead can lead to hurt, anger, and judgement.

Close-mindedness is usually caused by ego and fear. People that are close-minded are not open to new ideas, and they can be very critical and judgmental. This is a very unhealthy way to live and to look at the world. It's ok to have strong beliefs and self-confidence, but don't let that make you close-minded. Be open to new ways of living and thinking. When talking with someone that has a different opinion, try to truly listen to them and see things from their perspective. Try to see the world through their eyes. It doesn't mean that you have to change your beliefs or agree with them, it just means that you are weighing the evidence and coming up with the best possible solution or explanation. This is how the world gets better. This is how people progress and come together. This is how unity is achieved for all humanity. Start the conversation.

Debt

Too many humans are mired in debt. While some debt can be good in some circumstances, most debt is bad. Debt can encourage people to spend more than they can realistically afford. Being able to get something now without having to pay for it now can be very tempting. This can easily spiral out of control and lead to severe hardship. Having debt can prevent you from reaching your financial goals. It can tie up your money in monthly payments and interest instead of healthier options like savings, retirement, and pleasure. Debt can also cause health issues such as stress and depression. Having to pay monthly payments along with interest and fees can sometimes feel like you're being strangled. Once you go down the road of accumulating debt, it can be very hard to dig yourself out.

Some debt is usually necessary. Most humans can't afford to purchase a vehicle or home without securing a loan. This is generally considered good debt. In addition, many people can't afford to pay for college without getting a loan. This is also usually considered good debt. But other types of debt such as credit cards, lines of credit, personal loans, etc., are considered bad debt. Many people don't want to wait to buy new things so they buy on credit. This is a very bad habit to start. It is much smarter to save up the money for a purchase first instead of using credit. Emergencies do happen that may require buying something on credit, but that should be the exception, not the rule. Outside of emergencies, a home, a vehicle, or an education, you shouldn't buy anything on credit. Exercise patience, save the money first, and then make the purchase.

How do you stay out of debt, or what do you do if you already have substantial debt? Here are some rules to live by:
- Create and stick to a detailed budget. This should account for all of your spending.
- Live within your means. Simplify your life and expenditures.
- Don't impulse buy and only purchase what you need.

- Have one credit card for emergencies and online purchases. Don't use it otherwise.
- Payoff your credit card balances immediately. If you can't, save the money first before you buy anything.
- If you have multiple credit cards already, stop using them. Put all of your extra money each month towards paying off the card with the smallest balance. Once it's paid off, cancel the card. Keep doing this until you only have one card left. Pay off that card and keep it.
- Do the same thing for any personal loans and/or lines of credit.
- Start building up a savings account.

Debt is an easy trap to fall into. Use the above rules to stay out of it. Start the conversation.

Respect

Respect seems to be a dying idea in America and around the world. Humans just don't seem to care about anything anymore. They disrespect others with their words and actions, and they don't take care of things like they did in the past. Many people don't even respect themselves. Respect can mean many different things and be expressed in a myriad of ways. Accepting someone for who they are, even when they are different than you, is respect. Talking with someone politely and truly considering their words, even when you disagree with them, is respect. Treating others with kindness is respect. Having empathy for others and their life story is respect. Appreciating other people and their contributions is respect. Caring for the elderly and helping those in need is respect. Taking care of property and not littering is respect. Caring for the earth is respect.

Respect can lead to trust, safety, and happiness. Respect can build bonds between people and bridges between countries. Respect is the glue that holds humanity together. Without respect, there can never be unity. There can never be "we". There can only be "us" and "them". Some people don't act in a way that is worthy of respect. Respect is a two-way street. It has to be given and received by both sides. It is an agreement, a partnership. It is the secret sauce of life. Humanity must strive to act in a way that is worthy of respect. Start the conversation.

Positive perspective

Life can be really complex and overwhelming sometimes. There is no way to change that, but you can change how you react to life and its complexities. Life is a never-ending list of chores and responsibilities. Add in emergencies and unforeseen events and life can definitely keep you on your toes. A human's perspective is an incredibly powerful thing. Regardless of your perspective, you will still have to deal with all of the challenges of life, but your perspective will dictate how much stress, anger, frustration, peace, and ease you have along the way.

If you can keep a positive perspective, life will be much easier for you. The challenges you face will be merely irritating instead of life-destroying. When stress starts building up and your perspective turns negative, it makes things exponentially harder. Stress leads to frustration which can lead to anger. It can cloud your judgement which can lead to bad choices and consequences. It can steal your peace and introduce frustration into every area of your life. A negative perspective is like a cancer that spreads and destroys everything it touches. All of those negative effects can start to stack on each other and grow into even larger issues. Once a person starts indulging in a negative perspective, it can be extremely difficult to reverse course. Staying positive, even in the face of difficulties, is essential. Try to think about the blessings in your life instead of fixating on the problems. This is difficult for most humans and will require a lot of practice. Humans tend to obsess about the negative, and take for granted the positive. The trick is to reverse that, to obsess about the positive things in your life, and handle the negative events without the negative emotions. Try to stay positive in the moment. Count your blessings. Don't let yourself indulge in negative thoughts, and reverse course immediately if you do. Some of these ideas may seem cliché, but they work. They are not easy, and they require a lot of practice and commitment, but they work.

You will also want to broaden your perspective. When humans obsess about something negative, their perspective can become very narrow.

They only see the problem and exclude everything else. This can cause the issue to seem much larger than it really is. Take a step back and widen your perspective. Realize that life could always be much harder than it is. Accept that this issue will pass in time. Consider the blessings in your life. Try to help someone else with a problem in their life. Spend some time in nature. All of these ideas will help you regain a healthier perspective. Keep the lens wide and don't zoom in. Start the conversation.

Racism

Racism is one of the greatest failures of the human race. People may look different on the outside, but they are all the same on the inside. They are all created equal and they are equally valuable. Humans tend to divide people into different categories based on their race, political leanings, religious beliefs, what neighborhood they live in, what sports team they root for, their income, their education level, and a million other things. Humans use these categories to persecute and oppress each other. Everyone alive is part of the human race. They all belong to the same family. What would the world look like if people everywhere came together, supported each other, helped each other, and validated each other? What could be accomplished if people worked together toward common goals instead of tearing each other down?

Racism is a tragedy that needs to be acknowledged and learned from. It's like a cancer where different parts of the same body attack and destroy each other. In the end, there is only pain and suffering. Racism, in all its forms, must be rooted out and eliminated. It has a long and devastating history. It has hurt a lot of people. It has devastated a lot of lives. There is a lot of healing that needs to take place.

There is no easy way to move on from racism. Its reach is long and terrible. This can never be changed overnight, but it can be changed over time. Humans need to see each other as equals. They need to see that they are all the same. They are part of the same body, they are all intertwined. When a person acts racist against another person, they are committing violence upon themselves also. Humans need to learn from the past and create a better future, a future of inclusiveness. This will take a long time, and it can only be done one step at a time, one person at a time, and one moment at a time. Start the conversation.

Homelessness

Homelessness has become an epidemic in the United States. Experts estimate that nearly 600,000 Americans are currently homeless, and that number continues to rise. Homelessness has long been associated with mental illness and drug abuse, but the primary cause is a lack of affordable housing. The cost of renting has skyrocketed, and the rising costs of available homes have reached record levels. Wages have not increased enough for many people to afford rent, and this more than anything else has led to the surge in homeless Americans.

Governments have tried to address the situation with subsidized housing and temporary shelters, but this can be very expensive and there are too many homeless people. Rent continues to rise and this is just making the situation worse. Many states are raising the minimum wage, but if the cost of living continues to increase along with it, this won't provide the relief that is needed. Many people are moving to cheaper homes and apartments, but this has a trickle-down effect where the lowest income earners are being priced out and ending up on the street.

Homelessness is such a big and overwhelming problem that many governments are not sure how to solve it. The solution has to be multi-tiered and it has to start with building more affordable housing. The best way to do this is to create small villages of high-quality prefab homes similar to the company **Boxabl**. These homes have to be affordable, long-lasting, made with materials that do not degrade, efficient, and functional. The technology is available; governments just need to pass legislation to support it. Some laws prohibit these types of homes. Changes need to be made to not only allow these types of structures, but to embrace and encourage them. Creating affordable and long-lasting housing is the only way to start addressing the massive scope of homelessness. Start the conversation.

- As of 2018, the United States had more than 550,000 homeless citizens.

Marriage

The idea of marriage is a wonderful thing. Two people committed to each other, supporting and loving each other, with both people contributing to the union. Marriage is supposed to provide companionship, safety, and love. This picture of marriage is beautiful, but marriage is hard and it requires that both people engage, communicate, compromise, be worthy of trust, and be respectful. This can be hard for some humans to do, especially over a long period of time. Marriage requires that you work hard at making the other person happy. This can be very difficult as people change over time. When a person changes, this can cause friction, resentment, and a sense of not being close anymore. If the partner cannot change also or cannot accept the change, then this can lead to serious problems in the relationship. Human beings as a whole can be very selfish and narcissistic. These are bad characteristics to have in an intimate, loving relationship. Unfortunately, many humans are hard-wired with these traits. You can see how this might lead to a lot of issues.

It's easy being loving and considerate some of the time, but what about when you're tired, or sick, or stressed out? How about when your partner is moody, or stops taking care of themselves? How about when they change, or demand that you change? What about when one person stops caring, or stops investing in the marriage, or starts making their own happiness the main priority? How about when one partner gets lazy, or takes advantage of the other person, or becomes hateful? Humans are emotional beings and they can hurt others with their words and actions. Marriage requires that you trust your partner and be completely vulnerable with them. What happens when someone betrays that trust? Marriage can be very risky.

The idea of marriage is beautiful, but many humans can't or won't invest what it takes to make it successful. That's why so many marriages end in divorce. Marriage is hard and so many people are hard-wired to fail at it. There is a growing trend in the younger generations where they don't want to get married. They look around and see how miserable so many married couples are and wonder why they would want to risk that. Finding a compatible life mate is a brilliant goal, but the path is fraught with peril. The idea of marriage is beautiful, but it might not be possible in the modern world. Start the conversation.

Forgiveness

Forgiveness is one of the more powerful concepts in humanity. It can also be one of the most misunderstood. Forgiving someone does NOT mean that what they did was ok. It does NOT mean that it wasn't hurtful. It does NOT mean that you accept what happened or that you are excusing it. It does NOT mean that you will allow this type of behavior. Offering forgiveness does NOT mean that things can go back to the way they were. It does NOT mean that you have to keep that other person in your life. It does NOT mean that the transgression is water under the bridge. Forgiving someone is acknowledging that what they did was wrong, that it may have hurt you deeply, that you may remove that person from your life forever, that you may never trust them again, but that you are going to release the pain and hurt so that you can begin to heal. This is the only path towards health and peace.

When someone wrongs you, it can be incredibly harmful and damaging. Many humans hold on to these pains and they can start to take root in their souls. The pain and hurt can grow and infect every part of a person's life. It can sow seeds of bitterness and anger, and it can choke out the happier parts of life such as peace and love. If the pain is allowed to continue to grow it can eventually consume everything, leaving nothing but an empty husk of a life. Pain and grief can act like a poison, destroying everything it touches. Humans are good at hurting each other, and these hurts are very real and can cause serious damage. Left unchecked, this hurt can spiral out of control and destroy everything.

The only way for most humans to move on and avoid being destroyed by pain, is to forgive. Again, this does NOT mean that what they did wasn't wrong, or hurtful, or devastating. It does NOT mean that things go back to the way they were. It does NOT mean that you accept or condone what they did. It does NOT mean that you keep them in your life. Those decisions are all up to you. It does mean that you release the pain and hurt so that you can begin to heal. Depending on the severity of the transgression will determine how long the healing will take. It may require outside help such as a counselor or support group, or it may not. The path to healing may be quick or it may take a lifetime. The journey may be hard but it is definitely worth the effort. Your peace and health hang in the balance. Start the conversation.

CHAPTER EIGHT

The road ahead

What does the future hold?

Humanity is in a very unique situation. For the first time in history humankind can directly determine its fate. It has the technology and science to cure diseases, become a multi-planet species, usher in an age of Artificial Intelligence, reverse aging, save the planet Earth, and raise the standard of living for every human alive. Humanity has the tools to accomplish all of these goals, but does it have the ability to come together as a species to achieve these goals? To affect the lives of everyone on the planet, it will require everyone working together, lifting each other up, and inspiring greatness. Humanity is capable of amazing things, but can it set aside its differences long enough to realize them? Only time will tell. Start the conversation.

About the author

Michael Tyler James lives in Northern California with his wife and 3 dogs. He has been a part of the technology industry for over 25 years and specializes in Artificial Intelligence.